THE APPLES HUNG LIKE STARS

A SAPPHIC FAE RETELLING ROMANCE

GODSTOUCHED UNIVERSE

ALI WILLIAMS

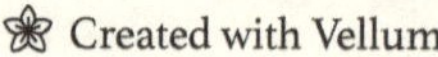 Created with Vellum

For Éire.

AUTHOR NOTE

Please be aware that this story contains references to death (off-page, centuries before the story), skin burns (on page, some explicit detail about the sensations), and kink (lots of it!). I hope I have treated Janet and Clíodhna's experiences and emotions with the care that they and you deserve.

1

———

Janet

I'm back again.

Standing on the side of the street, staring across the road at the neon-lit sign for The Golden Apple.

I've never been in, only done this weird staring thing, over and over, trying to pluck up the courage to walk across, open the door, and enter into what I imagine would be a darkened room.

You never know. The reception of a sex club might be well-lit.

Tam told me I wouldn't like it, that it's not the kind of place that nice girls go to, and ever since I've found myself back here again and again.

Because I might seem like a nice girl—I'm called *Janet*, for goodness' sake, you can't get more boring than that—but I'm not.

I'm not a nice girl.

I'm not a girl at all.

I'm a woman, and a woman who knows what she wants,

knows what she needs. And what I need won't come from some well-meaning, bumbling fool of a guy who doesn't seem to realise that I need more than a few pumps to get me off.

What I want are nights of losing myself so completely to dark desires, that I forget how to stand in the sun afterwards.

The light of the sign flickers, and it's almost as if it's a sign, as if I'm being called forth, summoned.

There are stories about the Golden Apple. About the decadence and the debauchery. Stories that have me squeezing my thighs together, feeling the throb of my clit, echoing. Stories of lust and violence.

People never seem to think that nice girls want the violence.

I want the violence.

Clenching my fists, I steady my resolve and take a deep breath. I've got this.

Before I can change my mind, I'm walking across the road, barely cognisant of the rain that bats against my hair.

Up to the door, and then three sharp knocks.

I wait.

The waiting is torturous. Agony. Almost as if whoever is waiting on the other side of the door is testing my determination to be granted entry.

Tossing my hair back, I attempt to adopt a look of nonchalance. I doubt I pull it off, but clearly something worked because the door opens silently and I have my entry.

The reception actually *is* well-lit. There aren't many people around at all, other than a bored-looking person who barely looks up as I walk over.

"Membership number?"

"I'm new." The words sound croaky, as if it's the first time

I've ever spoken aloud. It feels as though it might be, as though this is the first step into my new life.

They look up then, bemused by my apparent nerve. "You can't just walk in."

It's an exclusive sex club, of course you can't just walk in.

"I applied online," I say. "They said that I could come in for an evening? I've passed all the referencing."

"You brought your ID with you?"

I hand over my passport, almost fumbling it in my nervousness.

"You'll need a host for the evening. I'll ask someone to come down and get you. Do you want to put your coat over in the cloakroom?" They look me up and down again, an eyebrow raising in question. "There *is* a dress code."

I know that there's a dress code; I agonised over it for hours before heading out this evening. Tried on one outfit after another until I landed on this one. A short black velvet dress, its skirt floaty, and its neckline cut low enough to reveal most of my very amble bosom. It's not complicated, not even overtly kinky, but it makes me feel confident. Sexy. Desirable.

And I want to feel desirable tonight.

Slipping my coat off, I glance down and then up. "Will this pass?"

There is a softening around their eyes, and the receptionist smiles lightly. "Oh, sweet child, they are going to eat you up in there."

I bristle at being called a sweet child, but there's a shiver hidden under that bravado, a shiver at the idea of being eaten up. "I'm sure I'll manage," I say tartly, but I don't think they quite buy it, because they chuckle under their breath, and shake their head in amusement.

"Of course, you will."

My hands are trembling slightly as I hand my coat over to the cloakroom attendant, and take my ticket. There's a pause when I realise that I have no pockets to put it into. The attendant laughs softly, and gestures to me to turn over the ticket. There's a pin there, and I pin it to my dress.

"Harder to lose that way," she says. "Just be careful not to lose the dress."

Lose the dress?

I hope I won't lose the dress.

"Come now, Una," says a voice from behind me. "Her dress may get discarded, but it's very unlikely to be lost for all eternity." The voice is low, lower than any woman's voice I've ever heard before, and it resonates with me on a physical level, as if the tone has reverberated in my very soul, and awoken sensations I've never yet felt.

She is hauntingly beautiful, with red hair that falls to the ground, and pale skin that's almost ghostly in its complexion. On anyone else, it would make them look ill. She just looks ethereal, or as ethereal as anyone can in a tailored suit.

"Welcome, Janet," she says, spreading her arms wide, "to the Golden Apple."

2

—————

Clíodhna

She's delicious.

Her passport photo didn't do her justice, and the referencing checks we did, said nothing about rounded curves that I long to see bounce beneath me.

I should speak to Aoibheall about that. I think I'd like a little more warning when beauties such as this *Janet* are likely to enter my realm.

I cast my mind back to her referencing file. Tam had been her sponsor. Urgh. The man is mediocre at best. We'd almost rejected her application because he'd been attached to it.

Thank goodness we hadn't.

I walk down the stairs towards her, and she swallows. Adorable. "What brings a nice girl like you to my club?"

"I'm not a nice girl," she answers, her chin going up stubbornly. Delightful. I adore breaking stubborn ones the most. "I want to experience... *everything*. And I can't get that anywhere else."

"Tam was your sponsor. Did he not help you experience 'everything'?"

Her look is scornful. "Tam? Seriously? *No*."

That makes me laugh, and I'm not ashamed to say that I put a little bit of my power into it. Push it out until it makes her shiver. She bites her lip, an indentation in that plump fullness, and I want to nip and bite at her until she gasps into my mouth, as I know she will.

"Good to know," I say. I turn to Naoise, our receptionist. They're watching our interactions with unbridled interest and I shoot them a warning look. "Have you done the *other* induction?"

They shake their head.

"No matter, I shall attend to it myself." I offer my hand to Janet, and the sweet girl takes it without a moment's hesitation. "Come."

I lead her into the interview room off the reception, the room reserved for these specific inductions. We don't do them too often, not being keen on accepting mortals into our space all that often, but we make exceptions. And Janet is so utterly delightful.

"Take a seat?"

She sits, perfectly obedient. I've never craved such unspoken obedience before, preferring spirit that I can break, but this is intoxicating. She's doing as I ask because *she wants to*. Not because I've enchanted her—I didn't put enough power into my laugh for that.

"Janet, what do you know about the fae?"

"As much as anyone else in Ireland, I imagine," she says, before adding, "I mean, I wouldn't fuck with them."

"No, I wouldn't recommend that."

Janet looks thoughtful at my response. "You speak as if... as if they're real."

"You just said you wouldn't fuck with them."

"I mean, I wouldn't, but that's more because…" Her voice trails off and her gaze sharpens. "What's your name?"

I flinch before I can stop myself, and she notes it. "I can tell you what people call me here?" I offer.

"Okay."

"Clíodhna."

"Clíodhna, okay… wait. *Clíodhna*, Queen of the Banshees Clíodhna?"

It would appear that Janet knows a little more about the fae than most of the mortals in Éire that I've met in the months since the Veil fell. That could make this easier or more complicated.

"Yes."

She doesn't say anything for a long time, doesn't look at me, just closes her eyes and taps her fingers.

"Janet?"

"Shhh."

I'm not sure I've ever been shushed by someone before. It's a novel experience and I'm not entirely certain how to take it. If my sister were here, she'd go all glorious rage and demand to know who Janet thinks she's talking to, only Janet *does* know who she's talking to at the moment. That's why she's gone all quiet.

I sit down and wait.

Most mortals don't quite react like this.

Most mortals don't gain entrance to the club.

But every now and then we can sense *something* about someone. Something different. The Morrígan would call them Godstouched, though I don't know if that term quite applies to those who meet the fae. My sister Aoibheall thinks it does, although she thinks less of the Morrígan for abandoning us for Ciara—Ciara being the Godstouched mortal turned Pack that the Morrígan appears to have adopted as her own.

And that something was there in Janet's application. Aoibheall was going to discard it but I stopped her and I've been waiting waiting waiting for her to turn up since we accepted her. I've sensed her across the road, but this is the first time she's ever ventured inside.

Eventually, Janet opens her eyes and looks at me. "Can you lie?"

"That's a myth that's more attributed to—"

"*Can you lie?*"

"Yes." It's more nuanced than yes or no; there are things that can prevent us from lying—bluebells, for example—but for us fae who were once part of the Tuatha Dé Dannnan, lying isn't a problem for us.

"So, I could ask you whether or not you intend to hurt me, and you could lie about it."

"I could," I admit, "but I'm not going to."

Janet waits expectantly, and the tension in the air increases. There's a breathlessness to her questions, as if she's trying desperately to be logical, whilst also wanting to just give in to all the meandering thoughts her mind has ever had.

"I would not harm you. But hurt? Well, you're in a sex club, my dear, and I *am* one of the Dommes here. I suppose what I'll say is that tonight I won't hurt you... unless you ask me to."

3

———

Janet

I flush, my body aware of everything that Clíodhna's words promise.

So many people have promised me pleasure, but this? This potential for pain? This is what drew me to the Golden Apple in the first place.

I long to lose myself in the sensations that impact play might bring. My brain rarely slows, and the only times it does, I'm usually doing something physical, demanding, over and over in a pattern that allows my brain to switch off and rest.

I can't be sure that the hurt Clíodhna speaks of will bring me that peace, but I'm hoping it will.

As for the realisation that I'm speaking to one of the Tuatha Dé Dannan? I find that I'm not as surprised by the discovery as I might be.

"Should I be worried?"

"About what?" she asks.

"About the fact that you're some ancient being—probably immortal—and that I've signed a non-disclosure agreement to be here?"

She laughs again, that deep chuckle that makes me want to rub my thighs together. "I haven't been back for as long as all that. We were... gone." Clíodhna goes quiet then, her eyes distant. "Behind the Veil there are no sensations, no *anything*. All we want for now is to live with the abandon that you mortals embrace so eagerly. For myself? I take everything one day at a time, and for today, I want to show you around the Golden Apple."

My kneejerk reaction would be to beg her to do so, to pledge myself to her for all days, but I get a hold of myself and take a deep breath instead. "I would like that."

"You filled our questionnaire in the application stage."

"I did." My cheeks heat at the memory of it, deep searching questions about desires and fears and limits.

"Usually we would take that as your agreement, but for tonight, your first evening in the club, we prefer an opt in policy."

"Opt in?" I know what she means, in theory, but the realisation that I'm going to have to say, explicitly, what I'm up for this evening seems almost too overwhelming.

Clíodhna smiles reassuringly in the face of my panic. "Don't worry, we just ask you to refill out the form for this evening only. If you'd prefer just to watch, that would be absolutely fine."

She magics a form from somewhere—I try not to think too hard about how—and hands it too me. "Would you like me to talk you through each section?"

"No!" I squeak, and then clear my throat and repeat, more carefully. "No, thank you."

I scan the form. It's much the same as the form before

and I quickly tick through my limits, but then it comes to the things I want to do.

I want to try everything, experience everything, but in this first night there's a limit to what I can do, and a limit to what I probably should try for the first time.

Concentrating on not blushing too hard, I tick down a list of sexual activities, kissing, groping, fingering, cunnilingus, pause over fisting, and leave it for tonight. Orgasm control? Yes. Edging? Yes. Forced orgasms? Yes. Orgasm denial? No, I've spent too many years not reaching the heights of pleasure that I've only dreamed of.

And then the impact play list. I run my eyes over it, and speak up timidly. "Um, Clíodhna?"

"Yes, Janet?"

"About impact play?" There's a heat in her eyes as I speak the words, and I stumble over the next few as a result. "I haven't, I mean I have, but also I—"

Her hand reaches out to hold mine. It is anchoring.

I stop, breathe, and try again.

"I haven't really done much of this before, and I know I'd like to try, but I have next to no knowledge about implements. What would you recommend?"

Clíodhna looks over the form, her finger running down the list. "I have all of these, but if you're new, then perhaps we start with floggers?" From the way she's talking, she's making it sound like she's going to be the one flogging me. I'm okay with that.

I'm more than okay with that.

"I'm okay with hands, as well."

"Good to know." She smiles at me, a wicked smile that makes me shiver internally, and I try not to show it too much on the outside. I want to at least *attempt* to hold it together. "And where would you like such activities to take place?"

"Where?"

She points to a section on the form where a list of kink furniture lies. My eyes catch on the words 'St Andrews' Cross' and I can't look away. She follows my gaze and chuckles. "Shall I tick that for you?"

I nod silently.

"And the aftercare section?"

I don't know what I want for that, what I'll need to process such new experiences. "Do I need it?"

Clíodhna's face is suddenly serious. "Do you—*yes* you'll need aftercare!" She takes the list from me and ticks almost every box on it and shows me. Anything on there you don't like?"

I scan what she's ticked, and hide a smile. Cuddles, blankets, snacks, water, praise... These all seem like things that I would enjoy, with or without impact play. "That all looks great."

"Good." She takes the list and reads over everything else I've marked. "You haven't said whether or not you'd like a private room or to play in a public space."

"I don't mind." She looks doubtful, so I explain further. "I've never done public play, so I don't know whether it will add an extra layer of frisson for me, but the idea of it doesn't freak me out. I just don't know whether it'll heighten whatever's happening."

"I'm sure I can help with that." Her words threaten an experience I've never undergone before, and all of a sudden I'm so excited I can barely contain it. My fingers tip-tap across my lap, and when she glances down at them, I find myself explaining.

"I have ADHD, so I fidget a lot."

"ADHD?"

How to explain ADHD to someone who's immortal. I ponder the conundrum, before saying, "My brain works differently to most people. It's difficult for me to pause and slow down either my thoughts or my actions, so I fidget a lot, and take on too much at work, and sometimes don't realise that I need a break when I really really do."

"I see. And so you think that this might bring you some relief?"

Nodding, I venture, "I don't know that it will, exactly, but from what I've read, and what I've hoped..."

Clíodhna looks determined. "We shall bring you some relief tonight," she states, her husky tone warming me, and I believe her.

I truly believe her.

4

———

Clíodhna

When we finally set foot inside the club itself, I can't help but drink in each and every one of Janet's reactions.

She's chosen a quieter day to visit, a Tuesday, and so the club is not as busy as it might be at the weekend, but there are a good number of regulars here, and my sister stalks the upper dais. When Janet catches a glimpse of Aoibheall, she pauses and I find myself strangely beset by an envious feeling I've not felt much, but her face displays curiosity and not much else. Certainly not the waves of desire she's felt at my laugh. That soothes my ego somewhat, and I lead her further into the room.

There's a bar in one corner, which serves only non-alcoholic drinks, and I take her here first, demanding two glasses of water with a wave of my hand.

"Drink," I tell her, and she does, glancing curiously at me. "What?"

"Am I supposed to call you something else? Madam? Or Your Highness?"

Many in the club call me Mistress, but I find myself loathe to hear it from her lips. "I think I should like to hear you beg using my name," I tell her, and am rewarded with the slightest hitch of an inbreath.

"Clíodhna?" My name on her lips sounds like a prayer, and I've never wanted to be worshipped more.

"Exactly." I take a step closer and her mouth parts slightly. Pink lips beckon and I want to kiss, by all the Gods do I want to kiss her, but I won't take that first step. That first step, the beginning of the scene, needs to come from her. This time.

Next time I'll have her as mine the moment she steps foot through the door.

Her eyes fluttered closed and I realise that she's waiting, waiting for me to kiss her, for me to take her.

I lean forward and whisper in her ear. "If you want me, Janet, you're going to have to beg me."

That little gasp again and then this guttural moan that has my cunt clenching. "*Fuck* Clíodhna, just kiss me already."

I fist her hair, wrapping dark tendrils around my hand and pull her head back until her eyes fly open and meet mine. "Bossy little thing, aren't you? How do you think that's going to go for you?"

"Seems to be going just great," she murmurs, and she's already slipping into subspace. I can see it in the way her eyes soften and the tone of her voice hushes to a whisper. Damn if this woman isn't just made for submission.

"Beg me, Janet," and I don't need to put the slightest hint of suggestion into my voice because I know—I *know*—that she wants this more than any woman I've ever met.

"Please, Clíodhna. Please, do with me as you will."

And then I'm kissing her roughly, a bruising thing that paints all my desire for her, all my longing, across the touch of my mouth. She moans, open-mouthed, into the kiss and it's enough to set me on fire. I can feel my hair raising the way it usually only does before I keen.

When we break apart I know that I look as stunned as she does.

I've planned on taking it slow, building her up until she's in such a frenzy that the flogging would come as a relief, but now I'm looking at her shining eyes and I decide that there's no time like the present.

"Dress on or off?"

She swallows, but her answer is unfaltering. "Off."

"Go on then."

I watch as trembling hands reach the hem of her skirt. Janet sneaks a peek at me, but I keep my face blank. If I were a leannán sídhe, then perhaps I'd take this as my due, feed upon her desire, but instead I just watch, astounded by her unwavering trust in me.

She has no reason to be so trusting, and it brands her as the nice girl she disavowed herself as.

That's okay. I can make a nice girl bad.

As her skirt lifts, the tops of her thighs come into view, and then the hint of black lace between her legs when she pauses, and looks at me, a challenge in her eyes.

"Are you sure you want my dress off?" The hemline of her skirt dances, flashes of that black laces coming into view and then disappearing again.

Cheeky minx. "Yes." One word, so it can't be mistaken.

"Say please."

I growl, my displeasure and she squeaks and pulls the garment up and over her head in one swift movement.

"That's better, kitten. I much prefer it when you do as you're instructed."

She looks back at me then, eyes wide, panic filtering in. "I'm sorry, Clíodhna, I was only playing, I—"

I stopper her mouth with a kiss. It's not rough, but gentle this time. Reassuring. When I lift my head, her breathing has evened out. "I like seeing how *you* react, Janet, whether that's submissively or in bratty disobedience. You do not need to apologise. I would use the safe words we agreed upon if I needed." Her shaky sigh of relief makes me want to fight anyone who made her feel like this. Destroy them with my scream that could tear them to shreds.

"Thank you," she whispers.

I pull her flush against me, and run my fingers down her spine. Her underthings match, black lacy garments that barely contain her ampleness. Her breasts are threatening to overflow and the swell of her belly is soft against me. "There's a reason I called you kitten. You're unbelievably adorable, with a flash of claws when necessary. And I can always—" I lean in so my mouth is against her ear "—*always* put you in your place."

I feel the shiver that runs through her entire body, pressed as it is against my own, and suddenly I long to do the one thing I've never done here in the Golden Apple. I long to disrobe and feel her skin against mine.

5

———

Janet

I know that I ticked the groping box, but I didn't expect this.

This doesn't feel like what I've always thought of as groping, rough hands moving swiftly over my body, these feel like caresses. Even as Clíodhna threatens to put me in my place, she's coaxing responses from me, moans and gasps and shivers that wrack my whole body.

I'm trembling.

Trembling so much that I almost feel like I might fall.

"I'm going to affix you to the St Andrew's Cross," she whispers in my ear, each word feeling like a stroke against my clit, "and flog you for the entire club to see, and then I'm going to take you to one of the private rooms, and I'm going to fuck you. How does that sound, kitten?"

I nod eagerly, but she places a finger under my chin and forces my gaze up until I meet her eyes. They are red. "Words please, kitten."

"That sounds perfect," I say.

As she leads me up towards the stage, where a St Andrew's Cross is turned sideways on to the audience, I can barely believe what is happening.

I've never done something as wild as this. I dreamt of it, sure, but I didn't ever dare hope for it to come true. I'd give it all up for my fae queen, right now, and just be hers for more of this.

It feels like I'm high, my head feeling heavier than I've ever experienced, and it makes me pause just before we go up onto the stage.

"Janet?" Her voice is serious. "If you have changed your mind, we can stop. That is not a problem."

I know she means it, but that's not what's giving me pause. "My head feels heavy," I whisper. "I'm sure you wouldn't have... but I've never felt like this before."

"That I wouldn't have...? Oh!" Comprehension dawns on Clíodhna's face and she looks sad for a moment. "Oh my sweet kitten, no, I haven't messed with your mind. I wouldn't do that unless we'd negotiated such play, and even then... I have seen such games go too wrong to ever be truly comfortable with such things. No, this is subspace."

"Subspace?" I know that phrase, I'm sure.

She turns towards back towards the bar, and goes and grabs the water that I left on the side. The bartender nods at her, to confirm that they've been looking after it. "Drink this. I want you hydrated before we continue."

I drink and the soft haze begins to recede.

"When we play, subs often slip into subspace, and if you've never experienced it before, it can be alarming. We don't have to continue."

"No! I want to continue, I just didn't know what it was."

She laughs and my pussy is wet. "Good. Well then, up onto the stage, kitten."

I take her hand and step upwards.

There are people watching us below. I'd forgotten about them all until now, I realise, and the cross is set up in such a way that I shan't be able to forget them when I tied to it.

The cross is simple, with cushioned pads to protect my skin from the hard wood. I stand against it and I'm so short that Clíodhna has to attach extenders to the cuffs so that I can reach them.

She hands me a metal ball, and I clasp onto it, the coolness a nice surprise against my skin.

"If you need to stop," she says, "drop that. Use your traffic lights too, but the club gets noisy. I will see *and* hear you dropping that."

"Yes, Clíodhna," I say, and I'm feeling that haze come back. It's nice, comforting.

She takes one hands, and then the other, cuffing me and then attaching the cuffs to the extenders. Then with a deft movement, she uses her foot to open up my legs so she can cuff my ankles as well.

Everything goes quiet.

I mean, it probably doesn't in the club, but for me? Everything goes quiet.

The whole world fades away and all I can sense is Clíodhna, moving behind me.

She walks around to the front so she can see my face between the wood of the cross, and leans in and kisses me with such tenderness.

"Are you ready, kitten?"

"Yes, Clíodhna," I say. "Yes, my queen."

6

———

Clíodhna

Once she's tethered to the cross, I allow myself a moment to drink in Janet's body. She's plump—fat, mortals these days would call her, in a tone of voice that implies that they don't recognise a bountiful body when they see it. The swell of her hips, her stomach, overflowing as if the universe decided that we could never have enough of her.

She's made for this, softly braced against the wood, her arse rounded and offered up to me, even without her moving to do so.

Such a beautiful target area.

I caress her backside, dressed in black lace, and I'm momentarily tempted to tear them off her, but the masochist in me—usually silenced—wants to wait a little longer.

I want to earn the right to see her.

Touching someone like this, with gentleness, with reverence, isn't my usual modus operandi, but I don't usually want to fuck someone either. I want to fuck them up. But with Janet, I have very different intentions.

She is going to soar.

I turn to where the rack of floggers stands, opposite the cross and run my fingers over the tresses. The tails are different on each one; some are thuddier, while others have more a bite. Soft suede and even a man-made plastic... Each of them will have a different impact, will fall differently about Janet's body.

My fingers pause over one of the softer suede floggers. The tails on this are almost buttery, but it has some serious heft to it. This is what's calling to me. This is what I wish to use.

I take it off the peg and walk back to where Janet is waiting.

She has closed her eyes and I don't want that, I want her to open her eyes and to take in the adoring gaze of our audience.

"Kitten," I whisper by her ear, and her head lulls where it is.

"Yes, Clíodhna?" Her voice is breathy, and she's back floating in subspace, I can tell.

"Open your eyes, my dear."

She turns her head so it is resting on the pad and then only opens her eyes when she is facing me.

Brown eyes.

Deep brown, like the darkest bark of a tree.

Her eyes remind me of a time when I roamed Éire not in suits, and with a flogger in my hand, but rather atop a horse. Riding through forests, chasing through trees, making mortals dance at my every whim.

The Golden Apple fulfils some of that need, but not all.

I had not realised how much I miss it.

"Yes, my queen?" she whispers, and I told her to call me Clíodhna, but when she speaks like that, her words devotion, I cannot bring myself to resent it.

From her lips, queen sounds magnanimous, kind, merciful. None of them words that would usually be assigned to the Queen of the Banshees. I look out across the club and there are other fae there, some of them my subjects. They stare, eagerly awaiting the entertainment.

I almost change my mind and take her down, but—

"Clíodhna? Are you okay? Do you need to safeword?"

Her concern, even whilst trussed up for me, is touching.

"No, kitten," I say. "I don't need to safeword." I hold out the flogger for her to see, and her eyes go wide. "This is what I wish to use on you."

She swallows, and nods. "Yes, Clíodhna."

I kiss her. "Call me Clíodhna when it is just us. Now, in front of your audience, you are right. 'My queen' seems more appropriate."

Her smile melts that little bit more and the slight incline of her head seems more regal than any move I've ever made. "Yes, my queen."

"Now turn and look out at your audience."

She turns her head, and I can tell the moment she registers their gazes. Her entire body goes rigid, and I place a hand on her shoulder, grounding her. Slowly, the lines of her body soften until she takes another breath.

"Their eyes are glowing," she says. I hadn't noticed, how used I am to fae ways. From this angle, looking out from the stage, all you can see are eyes in the dark. Green eyes, mainly, and then the red of my banshee subjects.

"They are nothing to be afraid of," I say.

"I'm not afraid," she says, and though it's not quite a lie, it's not quite the truth either.

I straighten and look out at them all, meet my sister's eyes on the dais, and throw back my head and *keen*.

It's as heart-breaking a sound as I've ever made, and it echoes around the room, reverberating in every aspect of each being there. As one, all the fae bow their heads in acknowledgement, and Janet gasps.

"See, kitten," I say. "The only one you need to be afraid of here, is me."

She moans then, unwittingly, and I drink in the sound.

"What're your safewords again?"

"Green, yellow and red."

"Good girl," I say and she flinches. She actually flinches, as if she hasn't had anyone praise her like this before.

Unacceptable.

My Janet deserves to be showered with praise at every turn.

After she's taken her beating.

7

Janet

My entire body is humming with anticipation.

I'm so aware of every single step Clíodhna takes, walking round the cross, the air around me moving as she brushes past.

When she loosed that cry, I thought I might weep. Tears brimming, unshed. Now I feel like I might cry if she doesn't touch me.

I remember what she said, how she wanted me to beg, but at this point I'm so desperate for her touch that I don't know if I can use words anymore.

I feel untethered, floating, even as I'm cuffed to this cross. And I want it to change, I *need* it to change. Stillness for too long sets my ADHD brain on edge, sets me on edge, and that rarely has good results.

Eventually, *finally*, I utter a single word. "*Please.*" I imbue it with everything I've ever wanted, but had denied. Every-thing that I thought I'd never get to have, never get to experience. I don't need to beg her over and over, because it's all encapsulated in this single word. "Please."

The first strike, when it comes, startles me.

I'm not sure what I expected, exactly, but it wasn't this.

The thud of the tails as they hit my arse reverberate through me, setting my body humming. Awake and ready for more, desperate for me.

She goes again, and the sound the strike shocks out of me is guttural, deep. An "uh" that wouldn't be out of place on adult film set.

I've never heard myself sound like that before.

My eyes are closed again, but she leans forward and whispers in my ear. I love it when she does this; it's like her words have a direct line to my clit, and she speaks, I throb. "Eyes open, kitten. Look at how they all admire you."

When I open them this time, my sight has adjusted to the darkness of the club. The glowing eyes seem less eerie now, less like they've appeared out of nowhere from the dark. I can see the people they belong to, all languid, watching lazily, as I take Clíodhna's strikes.

They're all fae, I realise in a rush. No mortals would look at me like this. I think back to Tam, and wonder if he is fae too, but no. I'm not sure how, but I'm very certain that he is mortal. I cannot imagine him here, in this scene, watching on. He would rather be where I am.

"Are your eyes open?"

"Yes, my queen."

One woman... fae... whatever, leans forward, as if to watch my reactions more closely.

It's not the fact that I'm being watched that's heightening this tension. No, I don't think it's that at all. It's that I'm taking it for Clíodhna, that all of this feels like it's in celebration of her.

I'm making her look good, look great, and somehow that's what's getting me wettest.

That, and the next strike she delivers.

It's sharper, harder, heavier, and the "ooph" it pushes from my lungs is heartfelt.

"Green?" she asks.

I laugh, and throw over my shoulder. "I'm sorry, have you started yet?"

The entire room tenses, I can feel it, and I can feel something else too—a hunger. I have done something that has changed the mood and both they and I are waiting to see what the consequences shall be.

Clíodhna's laugh is low, and she drapes the flogger over my back and lets the tresses run down my spine. It feels like a caress. I know what's coming won't feel the same.

"Oh kitten," she says. "You're right. I hadn't started. I was going to warm you up first, but apparently my kitten doesn't like warm ups."

She leans forward and all I can feel is the material of her suit against my back, her hips, her crotch, thrust up close to mine. Even through the material, I can feel her heat.

She bites my ear. Hard.

It hurts.

This. This is what I crave. I let my head fall to the side, and she tugs at my earlobe, making me wince. "You want more, kitten? I'll give you more."

When she steps back this time, I feel the absence of her, the coolness of air against my skin, and all I can do is wait. Wait for what she's going to gift me.

The flogger comes flying through the air so vigorously I hear it before I feel it. The sharp 'crack' as it hits me, and I sense the room react. Leaning forward, watching everything that I have to give.

My head is spinning. This is... This is...

Yes.

This is what I needed. I laugh then, shocking myself and her with the sound.

"Is this funny, kitten?" Another strike, and I laugh harder, joy rippling out of me, infecting everyone with my delight.

"No," I gasp out. "It's not funny, my queen, it's everything."

I hear the audience gasp then, and murmur their approval at my response, and I can almost hear Clíodhna's smile in her answer.

"Good," she says. And then that's the last thing that she says for a while. The strikes fall thick and fast, and I lose myself in the sensations.

At some point I don't feel them anymore, or at least, not in the way I first did. It's as if I'm floating above my body, watching all of this take place. Swimming in a sea of sensations, that never threatens to quite drown me.

This is everything.

She is everything.

8

___

Clíodhna

If I thought she was in subspace before, it's nothing to how she is now. I keep on, moving the flogger in a figure of eight pattern that never falters. I've enough experience, and it's never felt as crucial as it does right now.

But then she slumps, her wrists pulling tight in the cuffs and I see that though she doesn't want me to stop, Janet's had enough. She's so far gone that if she needed to safe-word, I'm not sure that she could.

I hang the flogger back up, smile at her protesting whimpers, and then kiss down her back, palm her arse, and squeeze—just a tiny bit—to hear another delicious whimper.

"You're done, kitten," I say, and even though she says she isn't, I know better.

I undo her ankle cuffs, knowing that the wrist cuffs will keep her upright for the minute, and then scoop her up, using my free hand to undo the other cuffs.

And when her arms drop and she goes limp against, me I know I've made the right decision.

I don't even look back at the audience as I leave. I can sense their disappointment, but my sister's in a foul mood, I can tell, and she'll be more than happy to take it out on one or two of them, for everyone else's entertainment.

Janet is here for no one else but me.

No, that's not true.

She's here for herself.

There are a smattering of rooms off the main play area, and I head for the most luxurious. The one with a bed, for I want to lay out my Janet and feast upon her, and I want to do so in comfort.

She's still clinging to me when I close the door behind us, and turn on the dim lights. I go to lay her down and she shakes her head and holds on tighter.

"Kitten?"

"Nothing."

"Janet, are you okay?"

The tiniest, most imperceptible of nods.

"What colour are you?"

"Green," she manages to whisper, and her voice is hoarse, as if she's spent hours screaming. I manoeuvre her so that I can sit, hold her, and grab a water bottle from the bedside table. It has a built-in straw, so I don't have to wrestle with a lid, and I'm able to place it at her lips and order her to drink without much trouble.

She doesn't do so immediately, so I lower my voice to the threatening growl that I use with my banshee subjects. "If you don't drink..." I don't even need to finish the threat because she grabs it and starts drinking right away, gulping water as fast as her mortal body can handle.

She tries to stop, halfway through, but I don't move the

bottle away, keep it there until Janet sighs grumpily and continues drinking.

Once the bottle is empty, and I've shaken it to double check, I lean us both back on the bed so that we're laying down.

"How are you feeling, kitten?" I ask.

"Hungry," she says, and I'm about to sit up and find where we've put the snacks in this room, when she growls herself, an adorable noise. "Not like *that*. My queen, Clíodhna, I'm *hungry*." And it's only then that I discern her meaning.

She's hungry for *me*.

Good. Because I have been hungering for her since the moment I lay eyes on her, and I intend to eat my fill.

Her gaze has sharpened. She feels less melty and pliable, and more focused directly on me.

I pause, wait to see what she'll do next.

Janet reaches out, and strokes my hair. It's long and red, and I've been told many a time, rather creepy when accompanied by my keen. But right now, it's just hair, not a harbinger of grief.

"How do you fuck with all this hair?" she asks. "Doesn't it get in the way?"

I don't know how to tell her that I don't fuck, that neither Aoibheall or I do. That it's too messy, too bound up with fae politics. And that the mortals we fucked centuries ago put us off ever messing with them in that way again.

Because I want to fuck her, very much.

"I suppose," I say, avoiding the question. "I'll just have to pin it up." Her eyes widen as she watches me gather it all up and with a flicker of my fingers, magic it into a carefully assembled updo. "How about that?"

She looks like she's about to giggle.

"What?"

"'*What?*'" She imitates me, laughing. "As if you don't know."

I look at her blankly, and she sobers up.

"Oh, you really don't know. It's just that women in suits, putting their hair up like that, has kind of become synonymous with..." Janet's voice trails off.

"Synonymous with what?"

"With cunnilingus." Her voice is quieter than it's been all evening, quieter even than when she was in subspace. She's flushed and looks shy, and I'm a little confused because didn't she tick cunnilingus on her form?

"But you said that you were open to cunnilingus?"

Dark lashes blink rapidly, and she looks anywhere but straight at me. "I mean, yes..."

"Do you not want me to eat you out?"

"Oh no, I definitely do!"

"Ask nicely." The atmosphere has changed now, teasing turned dark. I like that flush, I like the way the swell of her breasts is touched with pink, and I want to see where else that pink goes.

"Please. Clíodhna."

"Good girl," I say, and grab her.

9

———

Janet

One second we're laying back, talking, and the next Clíodhna's hands are *everywhere*, touching teasing, caressing.

She pulls me to her with a roughness that mirrors our first kiss, but her hands aren't as harsh as the flogs that she subjected me to. But her mouth, fuck, her mouth is nipping and biting its way down from my lips to my navel.

She tugs at my bra. "Take it off, kitten."

"Say please," I tease her, but her eyes darken and I realise that if I don't take it off myself, she's going to rip it off me, and I like this bra.

I don't think I could feel more desired, but when my breasts fall from their perch, heavy, she curses and I'm hit with this sense of longing, the way I felt her grief when she keened.

She's not aware that she's doing it, that much is apparent, but the weight of her desire makes my head spin, and I reach for her.

"You're not touching me," I say, plaintively. "I need you to touch me, Clíodhna."

Her touch is drugging, in the best kind of way, and it is exactly what I need. Her fingers dance across me, painting patterns on the undulating waves of my skin. My body isn't small and delicate. I'm stocky. Fat. And the way she touches me, with such reverence, with such unbridled desire and longing for each and every inch of me, makes me feel seen like never before.

"I love touching you, cuisle mo chroí."

I almost stop then, almost make her take a step back and demand what she means by calling me beat of her heart, but her eyes are shining red and I realise that I don't mind. I don't mind because that's how feel too, as if we're two parts of a whole that have always missed the other.

When she breathes, I breathe.

When she feels, I feel.

I pull at her jacket, her shirt, tugging until buttons bounce off, flying everywhere, but I don't care. The touch of her hands, her mouth, isn't enough. I need to feel her against me.

It doesn't take longer than a moment for her to catch on, and then she sheds her clothes quicker than I could have asked for. Her breasts aren't as big as mine, her body more willow-y, but I don't love it any less.

I pull her down until she's lying on top of me, flush with my body, skin to skin, and I want to see a sheen of sweat upon her, I long to see her so driven by lust that she loses every inch of that control that she's clasping to her so very tightly.

So I bite her. I bite her shoulder, hard, leaving teeth marks and she fists my hair and pulls my head back.

"So, my kitten has teeth. Well, two can play at that game."

I don't know what she means, she's bitten me so much already. My skin is flushed with her bitemarks, from my neck to my ear to the tops of my breasts, but then she bites my nipple and I arch off the bed.

"Still good, kitten? Still green?" There's a taunting tone to her words, but I feel their sincerity as well.

"As if that'd make me safeword," I say, and entangle my fingers in the large bun that her hair is caught up in, urging her up towards me. "You could draw blood and I still wouldn't want to stop."

Her eyes flash red, and she nips at my lips. "I'm going to eat you," Clíodhna declares. I'm going to eat you all up, kitten, until you're begging me to let you come."

"I dare you," I say back, and I am, I'm daring her to enact every fantasy, every wish she's ever had. Because in doing so, she fulfils mine.

I loose her bun, and she moves down my body until she's nestled between my legs.

She breathes onto the gusset of my lingerie and I squirm beneath her attention.

"What's this? How dare it hide you from my gaze!" Hooking a finger into the fabric, she looks up at me and quirks an eyebrow in question. I know what she's asking and I nod.

She rips it.

And then there really is nothing hiding me from her.

Bracing her hands on the inside of my knees, she slowly pushes... so slowly that it feels like torture, and I open up for Clíodhna. I open up for my queen.

Her gaze on my clit feels like a caress, and when she blows gently across my pussy I can tell how wet I am.

I am dripping.

A lone finger runs up the inside of my thigh, and then up and over and around my clit, but she doesn't touch me, not even when my hips angle up and I follow her hand, pleading.

"Patience, kitten," she says, and her eyes betray just how much she's enjoying my neediness. But then all is forgiven because she dips her head and licks me.

If I didn't know any better, I'd have said that sparks flew when she touched my clit. I certainly jump, and her throaty chuckle pins me place. "Stay still, kitten," she whispers against my cunt and then sucks my clit into her mouth and I am undone. I am completely undone. More so than when she had me up on the cross, flogged in front of an eager and hungry audience. More than when she stripped for me. More than I ever thought was possible.

I feel everything dissipate into nothingness, feel myself begin to float away entirely, when she nips my clit and that brings me hurtling back into my body.

Gasping, I look down at her, and she raises her head and smiles, those red eyes glinting. "I'm not going to make you bleed, kitten, but you will feel exquisite torture like never before."

There's no reason to doubt her words, especially when her mouth is on my pussy like this. Clíodhna seems to excel in taking me all the way up to the heavens, and then back down to Earth with a thud again.

10

———

Clíodhna

Janet tastes like heaven, slightly salty, but with an undercurrent sweetness that I could glut myself on. And she's so receptive, so ready for me, that I find that I can edge her almost immediately.

And so, I do just that.

I start my mouth at first, lips and teeth and tongue, sucking and licking and nibbling, raising my face each time I feel her thighs tremble and start to shake.

I'm careful, because I don't want her to ruin. I want her pleasure to ebb and flow, to crest upwards before falling back down. It's all in aid of the eventual pleasure that I intend on forcing from her, over and over until there's nothing left for her to give.

But that won't be nearly as satisfying if she's not worked up.

She needs to be so close that she's almost crying, before I'll give in and grant her the raptures she so definitely deserves.

Her hands grasp at my head, fingernails grazing my skin, my scalp, almost as if she's massaging me. It's pleasurable and I hum my approval into her pussy. Janet jolts and shudders. "Clíodhna," she gasps.

I raise my head and rest my chin on the swell of her lower belly. "Yes kitten?"

She shakes her head, looking dazed, and swears at me. "Fuck you."

I laugh. "I'm sorry, would you like us to swap places so you can fuck me instead?"

She gulps and shakes her head again. "No thank you, please continue."

"Are you certain? I'm not sure that you want me to. We could take a pause and strike up a conversation instead if you'd like."

Her hand catches my bun and tightens round it. I can feel the hair tighten against my scalp and the sensation almost makes me purr. "More," she says, the order almost pleading. "More."

I take pity on her and dip my head again, this time to place a delicate kiss on the tip of her pretty pink clit. With my thumb, I brush it, marvelling at the way it peeks through dark curls. "You really are *very* pretty, kitten."

She's whimpering again.

I fucking *love it* when she whimpers.

"Pretty, and panting for me."

She moans again, and that's when I slide my fingers between her lips. Not all the way inside her—not yet—but teasing her.

Her hips start bucking again, in that movement that I've come to associate with need.

"How adorable," I say. "Do you want something, kitten?"

I expect her to snap at me, or to play fight, but instead she gazes down at me and says simply, "You."

I have experienced such purity of motivation before. Those who I fucked in the past wanted the kingdom that came with my patronage, wanted the power that came with blessing. They all wanted something *from* me.

They never wanted me.

And that is all that Janet wants.

I fill her with my fingers, and almost moan at the warm wetness of her. I beckon, slowly and curl my fingers until I can feel the raised bump that I know will bring her the most pleasure, press into it. She sits up, almost immediately, her legs trembling, and her thighs tighten about my head. I manage to move so I can look up at her, and she is stunned. Mouth open. Eyes wide.

"What are you...? What is...? How are you...?"

I stroke again and all words fall away, just as she falls, loose-limbed back upon the bed.

"Like that?" I ask.

She merely moans her acquiescence, and I continue. Her cunt clenches at me, and I add a third finger to the two already inside, revelling in how this makes me feel. It's not her submission that pleases me most—though it does certainly have its appeal—it's her full-throated enjoyment of this that has the most impact on me.

I am wet too, as if I've been submerged underwater. I can feel my desire for her at the apex of my thighs, just as hers coats my fingers. It's heady stuff.

I want more though, I want more from her, and as I start to fingerfuck her in earnest, her cries escalating in volume and pitch, I savour each moment.

"I'm going to... I'm going to come Clíodhna," she eventually gasps out.

"Not yet," I say, but I don't take pity on her, or ease up. "You're going to come when I tell you to."

Her face screws up, like she's trying with all her might to hold back a veritable tidal wave. "But... but..."

"Wait," I tell her, and shift so that I'm straddling her thigh. From this position I can finger her, grind against her and kiss her all at once. Leaning down, we're breast to breast and I can see the effort with which she's holding on.

Brown eyes meet mine, and in their depths I read everything I've ever been looking for.

"Now, kitten," I say, and I capture her cries with my lips as she comes apart. I can feel the waves wrack her body as she gives me everything she has. And just as she starts to come down, I pick up speed again and bite her ear, and she's coming again. The shocked look on Janet's face is sweet, so sweet, but soon it gives way to ecstasy as I coax orgasm after orgasm from her.

11

Janet

I am completely undone.

Clíodhna has undone me.

I don't know what there is left of myself to give.

I'm not sure if there's anything of me left at all.

I want to touch her, want to curl up in her arms and sob my gratitude for this great gift that *she* has given *me*, but before I can, the door to the room slams open and another woman storms into the room.

Clíodhna magics a blanket over me—I'm still not used to *that*—before spinning round to face the intruder. Her hair is no longer in its bun, but surrounding her like a force field, red and furious as her eyes. It should be alarming, but it's entrancing instead, almost as if I can't look away.

"*Sister*," the other woman says. She looks as different from Clíodhna as can be. Her skin is tanned, as if from basking in the midday sun, and her hair so blonde it almost looks white.

Clíodhna's hair lowers slightly, but she's still pissed, even I can tell that. "What are you doing here, Aoibheall? What do you want with us?"

Aoibheall glances behind her at me, and her eyes are full of something I don't quite recognise. Not quite grief and not quite anger, there's a longing there that's quenched when she turns back to my queen.

"Would you keep her?" The words are bitten out. "Have you forgotten yourself, Clíodhna? We cannot keep mortals here, and to let her go now, after she has tasted your delights..."

"I haven't actually tasted her... ahem... delights," I offer, but the two of them glower at me and shrink back beneath my blanket. "Cool cool. You guys just, you know, discuss me as if I'm not here."

That was clearly the wrong thing to say. Aoibheall rounds on me, "Oh hush, mortal. You know not of what you speak. You wish to throw your mortal life away for an immortal fae queen, who may discard you whenever she's done?"

Neither Clíodhna, nor myself, ever spoke of this going beyond this one night, but as I look at her, I know that I want this. I want *her*. "Sure," I say. "Why not?"

"Well," says Aoibheall. "We shall see." She looks at Clíodhna then. "Are you sure you want her?"

Clíodhna doesn't say anything, but Aoibheall clearly reads her answer in Clíodhna's face.

"Very well. On your head be it."

I'm not sure what happens next, but the blanket becomes very big, and very heavy, and feels weird upon my skin.

There's a strangled noise above me, far too loud. I go to

cower, bringing my hands up to cover my ears only I can't do so. I have no hands.

I have no hands.

What the actual fuck?

12

———

Clíodhna

There is a moment where I don't know where Janet is, what has happened to her, and it makes me ache the way that Aoibheall must have done after her loss of Dubhlaing, centuries ago. But then the blanket moves, and from it comes the largest snake I have ever seen. I reach round for my sister, to warn her, but she is vanishing out of the room, the door closing slowly behind her.

Its dark scales glint ominously and I'm about to trip backwards, off the bed when I notice its eyes.

Janet's eyes.

I freeze. Perhaps that is the wrong thing to do, for serpents are known for hypnotising their prey, but I don't feel hypnotised. I feel horror.

I should have known better.

Not that I could have expected this—because who could possibly have expected this—but I should have known better than to pay too much attention to a mortal whilst Aoibheall was in the club.

My sister, my beloved, infuriating sister, has been cursed to grief by the foibles of mortals. Her mortal lover Dubhlaing, who thought that he knew far better than a fae queen in the ways of the world, threw off the cloak of invisibility that she'd gifted him before battle, and died thereafter.

I never knew what she saw in him. He was handsome, true, but also far too fickle for my stalwart, loyal sister.

My sister who would do anything to protect me. The accusatory words she'd shot At Janet might have been about me treating her badly, but it had been to scare Janet off, to protect me.

The giant snake glides towards me, and its forked tongue hisses across my skin. I try not to shudder. I cannot abandon Janet now, just as Janet cannot escape this curse that Aoibheall has put upon her. The only way through for the both of us, is to hold on.

The thought haunts me, echoes of my urging Janet to hold on as I loosed her from the cross a mere hour earlier.

I have to hold on.

The snake does not look calm. It looks pissed, as much as a snake can look pissed. There's no way for Janet to speak, to make herself heard, and from what I've come to know of my kitten, that's the worst possible scenario for her. Trapped inside her head, no way to let her thoughts or feelings out.

Tentatively, I reach out a hand to touch the snake.

It snaps in my direction and this time I do jump back.

Mortals misunderstand what immortality means, much of the time. Gods and Goddesses can die, and fae queens even more so. And this fae queen is deathly afraid of snakes.

I curse Aoibheall. It's been too long since we've had a fight, and she always forgets herself if I go too long without reminding her that I, too, have agency and autonomy. I can and will choose what to do of my own volition, and whilst her input is often welcomes, it is neither necessary, not an order.

She needs to spend some more time in that catshape she so abhors.

The snake moves now, and the movements do seem hypnotic. I watch warily, and inch backwards when it goes to loop itself around me.

I fucking think not.

How much of this is the snakeshape, and how much of it is Janet is hard to tell. I wouldn't blame her for being pissed at me. I'd be pissed if I got turned into a snake without so much as a by your leave.

But shifting is an odd experience, even with hundreds of years of knowledge behind you. When I turned Aoibheall into a white cat, she spent the first week chasing after sunbeams and drinking milk.

I have never allowed her to live it down.

But now I see the downside of such an experience. Because a snake—especially one as large as this—would see me as food, and I would rather not be eaten by my Janet before I even have the chance to tell her how I feel about her.

But leaving is not an option.

I leave, and Aoibheall will shift Janet back and send her on her way, and I'd never see the mortal again. That is unacceptable. I shall not stand for it.

"Janet," I say, my words sounding oddly hollow against the opulence of silk sheets lit seductively. "Janet, it's me. Clíodhna. Your queen."

The last word registers with the snake, if nothing else. Its fangs come down hard on the coverlet next to me, and tear into the fabric. An anarchist serpent. Wonderful.

"Fine, forget the queen part. It's me, Clíodhna. You wanted me, you wanted all of me. Well, I'm here. I'm yours."

Cool scales slide across my skin and start to wrap themselves around my body. This is horrifying, nightmare-inducing. There is nothing I'd like less than to be held in the embrace of a giant snake—namely because I doubt I'd ever live past it—but there doesn't seem to be much else I can do. I cannot think of any other way to prove to Aoibheall that I am truly capable of making my own decisions, even if she considers them foolhardy.

Closing my eyes, I lean backwards, letting the coils of the serpent support me, and I give myself over to fate.

What's the worst that can happen?

13

Janet

I am trapped in the body of a snake. A monstrous snake, at that. I could see it in Clíodhna's eyes as she stared up at me, in unspoken horror.

That was unexpected.

I don't quite understand what it is that I could have done to her sister, to piss her off this much, but they fae are known for being changeable in their affections. One second, they can be yelling at you for sleeping with their sister, the next you're a giant snake.

All I'm trying to do is calm her, and I don't know how to do that in this form. All I know is that when she took me off the cross and I was so blissed out I didn't know where I was, it was her touch that anchored me, that grounded me, so that's what I offer to her now.

I encircle her, wrapping her in my coils, and hold her there, neither pulling tight or letting go.

I don't try to speak again—all that resulted in was snapping, and I doubt that a giant snake snapping its fangs is a sight anyone would like to be faced with. Turning my head, I glance down at the ruined coverlet.

My temper got the better of me when she mentioned her sovereignty, I must admit. It's one thing to not know what's going to happen, it's another to try and claim that as you're a queen, I should obey you. That's probably not what she meant, I can see that now, but in the moment it infuriated me, and the echo in my head that is more snake than human said strike.

I struck the bedsheets. That seemed the best move.

There is movement out the corner of my eye, and when I follow it, I see Aoibheall, angry below me. She is surrounded by more red-eyed fae, and they all appear to be taking an attacking stance.

I hiss my displeasure at them, and rock Clíodhna and my coils backwards until she is behind me.

If they want her, they'll have to come through me.

"Leave her." Clíodhna's voice is faint, but determined. "She's not hurting me."

"But sister—"

"*Aoibheall.*" She just sounds so tired, and I am sad, because I want her to rest. I wanted her to rest with me after those heady heights, and then I'd planned on pleasing her some myself. And instead, we're here. "Look at her coils. She is not tightening, just holding. She is protecting me in her own way, just as I'm sure you believe that you are protecting me in yours. Though *how*" —she mutters under her breath — "you think that forcing me to face a giant snake is protecting me, is beyond me."

I loosen my hold on her some more, and she shoots me a grateful look.

"She hasn't given into snakeshape thoughts, so how about you let this go?"

With a wave of her hand, Aoibheall does something thing and the mass of the snake, and the pressure it put on my mind since retreats, scales literally shedding until I'm sat naked on the bed, trembling.

Clíodhna turns on her sister immediately, but it's not her I clock first. It's the encroaching red-eyed fae, some of whom I recognise from the audience, earlier. They seem hungry now, hungrier than they did before, and the sharpness of their intentions hit me all at once. This time it is I who is tripping backwards towards the door, and I am out of it and running away before either of the fae queen sisters notice.

Everything in the club seems unnecessarily harsh: the lights; the music; the sounds of people laughing and playing together. It's nightmarish now, no longer seductive, and I can't tell whether that's actually what I think, or whether these hunting fae are inducing fear in me.

Who's that?

There's a voice in my head. Fuck that. I don't like that. I spin around wretchedly, trying to alight upon the speaker.

I know not, sister, who is that mortal there?

Which one?

There is a cacophony of voices in my head, one two three and I can't make out who is who and what they are saying and it is all far far too much before a startlingly tall woman takes my hands in hers and says, "I'm sorry for my sisters. They aren't used to sharing headspace with anyone but I."

Her touch doesn't ground me, like Clíodhna's does, instead it opens up a host of new voices inside my head, all shouting and fighting to be heard. There is one that feels slightly different for the rest and I hear it both inside and outside my head.

"Let's get you some clothes."

14

———

Clíodhna

By the time myself and Aoibheall realise that Janet is gone, and my banshee subjects with her, it feels like all is lost. I am tired of fighting to be heard every time we disagree, and this time it is more than I who has been inconvenienced.

If you can call being turned into a giant snake, inconvenienced.

It is she who notices first, because she falters, and then says hesitantly, as if she almost does not wish to say, "Clíodhna, your mortal is gone. And so are your banshees."

My banshees are wild things, too easily hungry for grief and sorrow, their keening gobbling up emotions like sweets, and I do not trust them with my fragile mortal woman.

I sprint to the door, looking round desperately for Janet. She is still naked, but the Morrígan of all people has given her a jumper. It dwarfs my Janet, who is as short as the Morrígan is tall, and as I hurry over, the Morrígan turns and snarls at me.

Her Godstouched mortal, Ciara, is by her side instantly, a calming hand upon the Morrígan's shoulder. But when she looks up at me her eyes, too, issue a warning.

One of my banshees steps a little too close to the three of them, and the Morrígan shifts into her wolfshape in a movement so fluid I can only envy it. Grasping the banshee by the scruff of the neck, she shakes and drops them. They stay prostrate on the floor, knowing better than to anger the Dark Goddess further.

"Ciara," I say, edging over to them, and then, "Kitten? Are you alright?"

Tear-rimmed eyes upturned in my direction and I don't care if the Morrígan wants to rip my throat out, I need to be there for my Janet. For my mortal.

I leap over the seating in a single, inhuman bound and flash banshee-red eyes at the goddess when she turns her snout in my direction.

"I'm so sorry, my sister is a *bitch*" —I don't bother to lower my voice and I can see Aoibheall rolling her eyes in the background— "but I wouldn't have you hurt for all the world."

But Janet doesn't seem to register my words. She looks shaken and dizzy, and keeps raising her hands to her ears, as if to block some noise.

"Janet?"

"Janet's Pack," says Ciara.

I'm confused. Pack? How can my mortal woman be Pack? Wolves make up Pack, wolves and wolf goddesses, the girlfriends of wolf goddesses, and apparently my Janet.

"I'm Pack, it does happen," Ciara points out, a touch snarkily. "But I understand your confusion. More than her being Pack, the thing we're struggling to understand, is how she can hear all of us."

"All of you?"

As fluidly as she'd shifted before, the Morrígan retakes her humanshape. "All of us. It is not something even I can do. She hears all the voices and thoughts of the Pack, and also that of my... sisters."

That's alarming. The Morrígan is a triple goddess, and her sisters are Badb, Macha and Nemain, the three different godheads that reside within her. I didn't know that anyone could hear them aside from she.

"Has it been that long?" asks Aoibheall, and I dare not look at my sister for fear that I'll attack her. She doesn't sound as if she is gloating though, merely sad. "Has it really been that long since we were last here that you have forgotten, sister?"

"Forgotten what?" I snap, my eyes searching Janet's face for some kind of clue.

"Forgotten the three trials we put our lovers through."

"The—but that is long done with," I say, confused. "Something confined to the times before the Veil."

Aoibheall's laugh is bitter. "If only. And because I triggered the first, the others will follow."

"But I can't help her with this," I protest. "I can't show her how to filter voices in her head—I've never *had* voices in my head."

"I have," says the Morrígan, and I'm not entirely certain what to make of that. She looks at me as if my voice is one of the ones in her head and scowls. "Stop being such a fool, Clíodhna. She is Pack now, and so I will protect her as if she were my own."

I know the truth of her words, and I hear it her voice, but it doesn't change the fact that I feel utterly hopeless.

The old trials were meant to test both the mortal and fae

lovers; test the mortal for fidelity and staying power, and the fae's ability to cope with feeling utterly hopeless.

There's very little that we immortals can't fix, if we put our minds to it. Sure, there are some things that are more complicated than others, but there are gods for just about every ailment on the sun—and the moon—so feeling help-less isn't something we experience all that often.

But I'm feeling it now. Everything about this situation makes me feel out of control, and if that's how *I* feel, then for Janet, who didn't even know that the fae were real before this evening...

I look back at my mortal, eyes closed, a sheen of sweat on her brow, and slump onto the seat next to her.

She doesn't open her eyes, but she does lean back into me and I can feel the relief radiate through her when I take her hand.

"It's gone quiet," she says. "You've made it go quiet."

15

———

Janet

Goodness only knows how we look, the four of us in various states of disarray, standing in the middle of a sex club.

It's the first clear thought I've had since being beset by the Pack voices, and it's more than a little welcome.

I tighten my grip on Clíodhna's hand and, when the voices abate, open one eye cautiously to take in the Morrígan and Ciara, properly this time. I know them now, because I am Pack. Well, I am kind of Pack; not quite in the way that they are, but Pack-enough that they accept me.

The Morrígan is taller than I fully comprehended, and I wish I could have seen her wolf when she shifted. She feels different, like I should be baring my neck in submission to her. She raises an eyebrow at me and I raise one back. I might be Pack, but I'm not her submissive.

That makes her chuckle.

Ciara is slight, beside her, red hair tied up into a jaunty ponytail that swings behind her. She looks worried.

I turn my head, and Clíodhna leans forward, her lips brushing my cheek. It's all that I can do to smile tiredly at her.

No talking. I appreciate the fact that none of them are talking. No one in the entirety of the Golden Apple seems to be talking, in fact. I look around, and most of them seem to be cowering away from the Morrígan.

I'm the Dark Goddess, and that puts the fae on edge, she whispers in my mind, and I can hear the laughter in her voice. *They can never be entirely certain what it is that I'm going to choose to do next. It's also why you can still hear me, when the rest of the Pack is blocked out by Clíodhna.*

It's a curious predicament to be in. Definitely a better one than being trapped in the body of a giant snake, or being hunted across a room by red-eyed banshees that look like they want to suck the marrow from my bones.

Do I want the voices to go away completely?

I don't know. It feels like a tether, a bond to other people, and that's something that I've felt has been missing from my life for a long time. And now I feel like I have two of those bonds, one to the Pack, and one to Clíodhna.

Clíodhna feels very still and very quiet. She's been still and quiet, especially when she was building the tension for me on the cross earlier, but she never *felt* still or quiet. She's like a livewire, zinging into action, taking up the air in every space she walks into.

Her sister walks into my sightline; the hair on my neck pricks up and both Ciara and the Morrígan turn defensively towards her. It's like we are all three in sync, and I can sense the disappointment from Clíodhna beside me. She feels left out.

I squeeze her hand. "If it weren't for you," I say, "I wouldn't bother with any of this."

She doesn't reply with words, but the answering squeeze of her hand tells me everything I need to know.

"Teach me how to shut them out," I say to the Morrígan. "Please."

She nods, and then literally shakes herself out of her skin. All of a sudden, I'm face with a very large, very red, wolf.

"I didn't know wolves come in that colour," I laugh, my nervousness showing through.

Her nose nuzzles up against my hand and it's okay, she's Pack. I recognise her. This time I don't hear her thoughts, I *see* them, like flashes of film, running through my brain. She's showing me strands of thread, all different colours and it takes a minute or two with being bombarded with the same images, over and over, but I get it. The threads are the different voices in the pack. That makes sense.

Then she sends me an image of a pin and I understand what she's meaning for me to do. I can pin the threads to a different part of my mind. They'll always be there if I need them, but they won't be overshadowing every minute of every day.

It takes longer than I'd like to put what she suggests into practice. Lots of thinking really hard in a particular direction, and twitchy fingers, trying to pull and move and coax things where I want them to be.

Most of the threads don't mind too much about being moved, but there are three that keep flashing in my mind's eye, as if they're pretty outraged at being pushed to one side. They're the first three voices that I heard, and part of me feels sad that I won't be able to hear them, so I bundle them around their very own pin, so that we can talk separately from the rest of Pack if we wish, and they seem to calm down after that.

Eventually, I'm able to disentangle my fingers from Clíodhna's, and test out all I've been doing.

Silence. Blessed silence.

I nod, and then collapse back into Clíodhna's arms, turning to bury my face against her.

She's still naked, hadn't even paused to put clothes on before she sped after me. Her skin is cool, clammy to the touch, and I can feel in her skin how scared she was for me.

"What could have happened?" I ask her.

Her face distorts, as if she doesn't want to answer, and then reluctantly she does. "Mortal brains aren't made to process that amount of information at once. I'm surprised it didn't break you."

I blink. This may be one of the only times when my ADHD might actually be mistaken as a superpower. Usually when people say that, it's a glib comment that doesn't consider the stress and trauma that comes from growing up neurodiverse in a world that's designed for the neurotypicals. But right here, right now? It seems fitting.

I came here because of my brain. I came because I craved the quiet relief from a never-sleeping brain, that I sensed submission could gift me. And in the end, it was that unrelenting brain—the brain that literally rewires itself when it can't do something—that helped me survive. I'm so used to processing all of the sensory input, all of the time, that the whole of Pack in my head? Not a problem.

Looking around, I catch Aoibheall's eye. "Okay, you started this. I've got three trials to overcome? What's next?"

16

————

Clíodhna

Aoibheall's grudging respect for Janet is as apparent as Ciara and the Morrígan's bemusement. No one in the club knows quite what to make of my mortal, and that is quite satisfying.

Almost as satisfying as the fact that she seems to be quite the mouthy, confident thing when speaking to anyone but me.

I mean, she's mouthy and confident when she's with me, but she's also a deliciously melty little thing as well, and I'm glad that I'm the one who gets to entice that out of her.

Janet stands, and even my banshee subjects take a step back. There's something *more* about her now. Maybe it's the fact that she holds all the voice of a magical Pack in her head, or perhaps it's just her. That this whole experience has tapped into a magical vein that's been hidden deep within her soul.

She's Godstouched.

I consider Ciara for a moment, though not for too long,

as the Morrígan tends to get a tad overprotective of her own mortal. She has a similar feel. It's almost as if whatever makes them mortal has somehow been indelibly changed.

I'm all in favour of it.

"Well?" Janet demands of my sister. "What's next?"

"I don't know," she says, shrugging helplessly. "I set the trials in motion, but I don't know what comes next. I've never known."

We all stand there, as useless as new-born lambs. It's as if all our legs have been cut out from beneath us. All of us, except Janet.

"There's got to be *form*," she insists. "I'm not going to just stand around and wait for something drastic to hit me. That seems ridiculous." She stares at us all. "Aren't you all supposed to be immortals? Don't you have some kind of control over fate?"

That makes us laugh. Even Aoibheall.

"If that were the case," she says, "do you think we'd have been caught behind a Veil for centuries?"

Janet exchanges a glance with Ciara. "I'm not wrong though, am I?"

Ciara nods. "You're not wrong at all, but I'm probably not the best person to ask. I didn't start forging my own fate until Red here came into my life." There's a grief in her eyes that calls my keening to the tip of my tongue, but I fight to get it under control. Whatever Ciara has been through, she doesn't need me calling her grief into being.

"Fine." There's that stubbornness in her. Her chin goes up and her dark eyes flash with fire. "If you're not going to do something about this, then I will. Clíodhna, what do you hate the most?"

"Other than snakes, you mean?"

Aoibheall has the grace to look abashed at that.

"Not as in what do you fear; what do you dislike the most? What hurts you?"

My eyebrows go up, but I see what she's getting at. The first trial had been about her losing control, and me facing my own fears. The second had been her encountering great magic and prevailing, and me giving up all control over the situation, and coping with it.

The third would have to comprise of some physical feat.

"Iron." The Morrígan's voice is low and hisses come from the surrounding banshee. "You fae hate iron the most."

There's truth in her words, for what good that will do us, for there's no iron in this club. No self-respecting fae would walk through the doors if there were.

"I've got some in my truck," offers Ciara.

Everyone looks at her, horrified. "Why would you have iron in your truck?" I demand.

"You mean, aside from the fact that most cars are made from iron in some form or another? Red made me keep a chain of iron links in the back."

All fae gazes turn to the Dark Goddess accusatorily. She shrugs. "just because I get on with some of you, doesn't mean that I trust my Ciara with you. You've all got a pretty twisted sense of humour at times."

She stares each fae down and we all drop our eyes, even me. I might have banshee-red eyes that glow when I'm angry, but she's a triple goddess, *the* Dark Goddess. There's no challenging her.

"I'll go get it from the truck," she says, and then pauses and looks back at Janet. "Get yourself up on that cross; we'll lash you to it with iron chains. There isn't much else that the universe can throw at the two of you that would top that."

17

———

Janet

There isn't much time for me to truly comprehend what's about to happen. For the second time this evening, I'm to be bound to a cross on a stage in a sex club.

And for the second time tonight, Clíodhna is going to untie me, and make me hers.

She's gone pale though, paler even than where I heard her keen.

I step towards her. "Are you okay?"

She nods slowly. "I... I don't think you know what this is going to be like. As a trial is a rough one, not just for me, but for you as well. If we're going to pass it, if we're going to persuade the universe that we get to be together, then we're both going to suffer."

That's alarming. "I'm going to suffer?"

"Iron is... not great for fae. It burns. Literally. It won't physically hurt you, but it'll likely be an unpleasant experience. And if you can't take it, that's okay, Ciara and the Morrígan can untie you."

I didn't expect that. I didn't realise how much it would physically hurt her. "I don't want to hurt you—I don't want to *harm* you. Is it worth it? Is *this* worth it?"

For all that we've gotten caught up in this weird trial thing, we haven't even known each other for a full day. She's going to test the limits of her body for what? A quick fuck?

It's as if she's the one who can hear voices because she gathers my face in her hands and kisses me sweetly. "Don't think like that. You are worth it. You are worth *all* of it. You are sweet and stubborn and delicious when you submit, and I'm not above saying that I want you so very desperately."

"But you've had me." I'm scared, I realise. Scared that when this is all over, she'll decided that she doesn't want me anymore. "And at some point, the novelty of a mortal lover will wear off."

"It's not the novelty I crave," she says, and then she speaks my words right back to me. "It's you. I want you."

We stand there, anchored to each other in the middle of a sex club, people running around, talking shouting, calling, and it's as if the place is deserted and there's no one there but us. We kiss, casting everything else aside, losing ourselves in the touch of each other, the feel of each other.

Clíodhna's lips are cool against mine, insistent, and this is unlike any of the kisses that have come before it. This is a kiss brimming with hope, potential.

Someone clears their throat behind us, and the Morrígan stands there, a mass of iron in her arms. Clíodhna hisses and steps backwards, and I can see her hair rising in that red mass.

The club is now nearly as deserted as I'd imagined it. Just the Morrígan, Ciara, Clíodhna and I. Aoibheall comes striding back into the room, calling over her shoulder some instruction to the receptionist, and stops dead.

"Move it to the stage. Please," she says, and her tanned skin has paled until it's almost the same colour as her white-blonde hair. The Morrígan takes a step forward, but Ciara shakes her head and takes the iron chains from her.

"There's enough pressure all round; I'm not sure that Clíodhna would appreciate watching you wrap Janet in iron right now."

"Clíodhna would certainly *not* appreciate that. Especially dressed in your fucking jumper."

I roll my eyes and pull the jumper up and over my head. Everyone is startled, and the Morrígan averts her eyes. "As if you haven't all seen this before. This is a sex club, remember?"

Ciara clears her throat. "It's our first time here; we're not exactly regulars."

"Oh." I go to put it back on, but instead turn and look at Clíodhna. "Will seeing me, seeing all of me, help? Will it be good motivation?"

Clíodhna doesn't answer, her jaw ever so slightly slack. It's nice to know that even after all that has transpired this evening, I have the ability to render her speechless.

"I think that's a yes," interjects the Morrígan, dryly. "As for the rest of us, we'll avert our gazes. Ciara, you're okay to do the tying?"

She nods, but there's something that she's not saying. I reach for the pale blue thread that I've come to identify as hers, and I ping it mentally, as if plucking it with my finger. She looks up sharply and meets my eyes.

There are unshed tears in hers, and I almost tell her to forget it, that I don't want her to cry, but then I see Clíodhna standing behind her, looking so very very lost and my resolve hardens.

"We can do this bit together," I say. "You're not doing anything that I don't want, and if things go wrong you'll untie me, yes?"

She nods. I feel a wave of protection and I look at the Morrígan angrily.

The person who's put those tears in her eyes? He's been dealt with, she answers in my mind. *You have my word.*

I nod and step towards the stage, Ciara following me.

The cross is angled, so I'm not flush out to the audience, no matter which way I turn, which works for me. I lean back and face outwards. No cuffs for my wrists and ankles this time, only iron will bind my body to the cross.

I've never had such heavy links against my skin before.

"I'm not going to bind you so tightly that you'll panic," Ciara says, but there has to be some tension, or they won't hold up."

"I understand."

They're cold. So cold. My body shivers and I can feel goosebumps raising across my skin. Clíodhna takes a step forward, a strangled objection lingering on her lips. Her hair is a mass of red fury now, and her eyes are so deeply red I can see them from here.

"I'm alright," I say, but I can tell that she doesn't quite believe it. It's too much for her to grasp, to comprehend, when I'm bound tightly in the one material she hates the most.

Ciara makes deft work of the binding, squeezes my hand and steps back.

I look at Clíodhna. "Come get me."

18

Clíodhna

I can't stop myself from admiring how good Janet looks, bound up in chains. In any of situation, I'd pause and dwell on that, on the indentation it's making against her stomach, how when I pull it away, it'll pattern her skin with shapes and reminders of how she's been bound for me.

But this is not rope.

This is iron.

I have not touched iron in centuries. Haven't wanted to. Haven't needed to.

But now it is the thing that could save me and damn me.

I take a step forward and the hairs on my arms go up. I'm not going to be able to accomplish anything if my banshee nature steps in. Sweeping my mess of hair upwards, I force it into a bun, and pin it with even a physical pin now, just for good measure. I dressed, whilst Ciara was binding my Janet, my theory being that the less skin on display, the less there is to burn.

Time to test out that theory.

Another step forward.

Everything in me is urging me to step back, to turn and walk in the other direction as quickly as I possibly can. It's not just that there's iron, it's that there's just so fucking *much* of it. The Morrígan has enough here to destroy an entire army of fae, if she so wanted. At some point I intend to have a fairly strongly word conversation about that, Dark Goddess, or no Dark Goddess, but right now I'm just focused on inching my way forward towards Janet.

She smiles, encouragingly at me, and I take several steps all in a rush until I'm standing in front of her.

I can feel my skin heat, and the hair on my forearms starts to burn. Tiny sizzling pinpricks all over. It's not over-whelmingly painful. Yet.

"I love you," Janet says. My eyes meet hers and I take one more step and I'm so close to the iron I might burst into flames. But I don't care because all I can hear is *I love you I love you I love you* on repeat in my brain.

"How can you possibly...?"

"I don't know," she says, calmly. "I don't know how it's even possible to love someone after knowing them for such a short amount of time, but I have never felt so cherished. I have never felt so safe. I have never felt so loved."

She's not waiting for me to say it back. She's just saying it because it is her truth, and because she thinks I need to hear it.

I do.

I've never heard those words before. Something in me heals, even as I'm about to catch light.

Reaching out, I grasp the first chain. It sizzles beneath my hands and the scorching heat catches me by surprise. I jump back and look at my hand.

The skin on my palm is red raw. I roll up my sleeve and

the skin under my shirt sleeves is bright pink also, and that hadn't even touched the iron.

This is not going to be an agreeable endeavour.

I take a deep breath and grasp the chains again. The smell of burning flesh fills the air, and I try to hide my whimpers of pain by clanging the chains together loudly.

"I see you," she says, and I can see pain painted across her features. She can tell how much this hurts, how much I'm willing to put my body through for her.

Ciara has done far too good a job of binding my Janet, and that makes it harder yet. Shooting pains shatter my concentration, and I have to drop links occasionally, and start untangling them from the beginning more than once.

"This better be enough for the universe," I mutter, and she laughs, not at my pain, but at my stubbornness. "We are not going through another trial after this."

"As if being with you won't be a trial in itself." Her eyes are bright with mischief and I can't help myself, I lean in to kiss her.

Heat sears my flesh, branding my endeavours on my skin, and she winces, nudging my head back, away from the iron.

"Please hurry, darling," she says. "I don't like that you're in pain."

I wrestle with the last few links and then step back, watching as they tumble to the ground and Janet—my Janet —steps free.

She runs straight to me, calling to Ciara and the Morrígan and my sister to grab the first aid kit, and doesn't stop to kiss me. Her hands go straight to the buttons of my shirt and she rips it open.

I chuckle, but it's a pale imitation of my usual laugh. "Couldn't wait to get me naked, eh, kitten?"

"Oh, hush yourself," she says, revealing the extent of the damage. "You just concentrate on healing." She looks up to the sky and makes a declaration that I feel all the way down in my toes. "We are done now. You try and send us any more trials, I'll take them and shove them up your immortal arses, I don't care how great and powerful you are. You just leave us be."

Aoibheall and I exchange glances. It's never wise to tempt fate when it comes to the gods, and my little mortal has pretty much thrown down a gauntlet to anyone who was paying a passing interest. But then the Morrígan steps up onto the stage, and places her hand on my Janet's shoulder.

"Well said, Janet." She too looks upward, and when she speaks it is not with one voice, but with three. "*The trials are complete. Let any who dare challenge the word of Badb, of Macha, of Nemain, of the Morrígan.*" Her voice is a hoarse scream by the time she reaches her own name, and the very air itself feels as though it's thrumming with expectation.

But then Ciara, slips her hand into the Morrígan's, and she turns back into the tall woman she usually appears as. But it's hard to forget the look of a Dark Goddess, three in one, daring an entire pantheon to challenge her.

I'm glad that she's on our side.

19

———

Janet

We're both naked, Clíodhna and I, and I wish more than anything that we were alone. I long to bathe each burn, to kiss it, and watch it heal beneath my touch, but I know that first aid is far more beneficial in moments like this.

"I cannot quicken your healing, sister," says Aoibheall, and I eye her nervously. I'm still not confident in where I stand with her just yet. "But I can offer you my congratulations for passing the trials." She turns to me and I fight not to take a step back. "Not many would have succeeded as you, and many more have failed, so for that you have my respect."

I'll take the respect of a fae queen, no matter how begrudging.

But I want *my* fae queen more than I want to talk to her sister. "Clíodhna?"

"Yes kitten?" She sounds oh so very tired, and I want to gather her up and make her rest.

"You're coming with me." I nod towards the others, and then turn away, clearly dismissing them. If I'm to be the a fae queen's lover, I'm going to have to project confidence, and I'm starting on it early.

I lead her over to the room where she ravished me earlier that evening—it seems like forever ago now— and as I close the door behind us, I drop to my knees.

Clíodhna sits heavily on the bed and looks at me.

The burns have not yet faded, and her hands are bandaged because they were so raw it almost made me cry to look at them. But she is mine, and I am hers.

I sit at my feet and rest my head gently against her knees, avoiding tender areas. I know she can't stroke my hair, can't really even touch me the way I know she longs to, but the position brings comfort to us both.

We've been so busy wrestling with these trials, that I'd forgotten what it felt like to just be with her. My brain quiets, and the world and all its troubles melt away into nothingness.

There is nothing in all of existence but us, of this I am sure.

"Come," my fae queen says. "Come kitten, Janet, my love. Come to bed."

"Yes," I say. "Yes, my queen."

The End

AOIBHEALL'S BOOK IS NEXT

My sister never came home from her night at the Golden Apple, and as cautious as I am... I'm just as loyal. So, into the Dommes' lair I go.

But when I see Aoibheall, all raging beauty and fury wrapped up in one, I find myself giving over to the pleasure that her eyes promise.

Welcome to the Godstouched Universe, where the Gods interfere in the lives of mortals, magic leaks back into our world, and love conquers all.

Their Fruits like Honey is a sapphic Goblin Market retelling.

READ THE MORRIGAN AND CIARA'S STORY IN TWISTED PRIDE

Chase Me In the Woods

Ciara: I'm not known for being social. I live in a cottage on the outskirts of Dingle—the most easterly point of Ireland—keep myself to myself, and try not to let the trauma of my past inform my present. But when that past comes back to haunt me, the one thing that keeps me safe is the red wolf who sleeps by my door.

The Morrigan: The Veil between worlds is gone, and men are causing as much chaos as ever they did, and one such man is haunting the girl in the woods. As Dark Goddess I could destroy him, I want to destroy him, but I'll watch in my wolfshape, and guard the girl who feels like Pack.

Welcome to the Godstouched Universe, where the Gods interfere in the lives of mortals, magic leaks back into our world, and love conquers all.

Chase Me in the Woods is a sapphic Little Red Riding Hood retelling where the woodcutter gets his comeuppance, and the wolf goddess gets eaten out.

ALSO BY ALI WILLIAMS

GODSTOUCHED UNIVERSE

Forged in Flames: A Dragon Shifter Romance

Value in Visions: A Sapphic Psychic Romance

Married in Moonlight: A Sapphic Psychic Wedding

The Apples Hung like Stars: A Sapphic Fae Romance

Their Fruits like Honey: A Sapphic Fae Romance

Lure Me to the Deep: A Sapphic Mermaid Romance

Chase Me in the Woods: A Sapphic Shifter Romance

Catch Me in the Dark: A Sapphic Samhain Romance

Nix and Tell: A Sapphic Fae Romance

Never Nix Up: A Sapphic Fae Romance

Don't Give a Nix: A Sapphic Fae Romance

EROTIC ROMANCE

The Softest Kinksters Collection: An Erotic Romance Collection

Kink the Halls: A Sleeping with my Ex's Mum, Lesbian Christmas Romance

Flogging Faith: A Submissives of Rawhide Romance

STUFFIE HOSPITAL BOOKS (AS ELLIE ROSE)

A Little's Unicorn (Lillie and Aiden's book)

A Little's Reindeer (Georgie and Warren's book)

A Little's Lion (Kacie and Dex's book)

A Little's Patchwork Bear (Ralphie and Nate's book)

A Little's Witchy Bear (Rylie and Eve's book)

A Little's Engagement (Ralphie and Nate's sequel)

A Little's Monster (Christie and Dana's book)

A Little's Dino (Archie and Rebecca's book)

A Little's Elephant (Frankie and Grey's book)

A Little's Owl (Darcie and Richard's book)

A Little's Pegasus (Beanie and Abigail's book)

STUFFIE HOSPITAL LONDON BOOKS (AS ELLIE ROSE)

A London Little's Llama (Billie and Mark's book)

A London Little's Moo (Tillie and Alex's book)

A London Little's Dragon (Jamie and Marian's book)

A London Little's Giraffe (Mossie and Daniel's book)

A London Little's Penguin (Rubie and Anna's book)

A London Little's Pom Pom (Rosie and Eloise's book)

A London Little's Bunny (Essie and Ben's book)

A London Little's Octopus (Charlie and Leon's book)

A London Little's Tiger (Susie and Briana's book)

THE LITTLES' MARKET BY THE SEA BOOKS (AS ELLIE ROSE)

Isla (Isla and Rachel's book)

Emma (Emma and Bryn's book)

Liv (Liv and Cat's book)

Sage (Sage and Lily's book)

Tess (Tess and Willow's book)

Reba (Reba and Kirby's book)

Nicole (Nicole and Violet's book)

Brooke (Brooke and Jenny's book)

Morgan (Morgan and Rose's book)

Wyn (Wyn and Tel's book)

River (River and Alice's book)

Aubrey (Aubrey and Helen's book)

Skylar (Skylar and Gabrielle's book)

Rawhide Ranch Books (as Ellie Rose)

Mandi's Little Mother's Day (Mandi and Amelia's book)

ACKNOWLEDGMENTS

The Godstouched are back!

Janet and Clíodhna—like The Morrígan and Ciara, and Lí Ban and Niamh—were born out of a trip to Dingle back in 2022. It was my first writing retreat, with Amy Andrews and Pippa Roscoe, and we spent as much time exploring the Irish countryside as we did writing. I fell in love with it. My grandmother is Irish, and I've worked with Irish goddesses for years, but that was my first time visiting Éire herself. It was magical. And so, I moved away from the South Downs to the furthest point of Ireland for my next few books. I hope you'll follow these characters in and out of each other's lives.

This book owes so much to my friends who have cheered me on—and cursed my chaotic goblin nature—at every stage. Thanks go in particular to Rayanna Jamison and EJ Frost, for sprinting with me for hours on end, so I could meet my deadlines. EJ is used to my bullshit at this point, but I think it was a steep learning curve for Ray! Also, to Niki Roge, who has adapted her own unique motivational style for my neurospicy behind. Thank you for the encouragement and praise.

As ever, Meka James, Karmen Lee, Rae Shawn, K and DAnn Williams have my appreciation for calling me out, yelling at me kindly, but always being there. You all have seen me through since the last Godstouched books, and I'm glad that they're back.

To Eden Bradley, Allysa Hart, Stella Moore, and Jami Dabney. Your friendships have helped sustain me over these last few months, and brought light when I've struggled. I am extremely grateful and lucky to have you all in my life. I hope I bring you some amusement with silly voice notes in my very British accent.

And to my Abi, who is curled up asleep next to me as I type this. I couldn't have written the kind of partner you are for me, and as wonderful as all my characters are, they pale into insignificance next to you. Thank you for loving all of me: the chaos, the anxiety, the silliness. I have never felt more cherished.

Now we come to you, dear reader. I don't know how you found yourself here, in my Godstouched universe, but I hope these exploits have diverted you from your troubles, if only for a short while. Thank you for reading my book. May you always find where you left off reading, and may your kindle never run out of charge.

ABOUT ALI

Ali Williams is a sapphic AuDHD author who writes intensely kinky paranormal romances as Ali, and fluffy and spicy age play romances as Ellie Rose.

Her PhD research focuses on the intersection between queerness and kink in feminist romance, and her sell-out online lecture series, Romancing the Discourse, discussed everything from how erotic romances use kink as liberation, to how paranormal romance can degender agency.

When she's not writing, she can invariably be found reading tarot, traipsing round the South Downs with her girlfriend, or playing boardgames with her queer, kinky, found family.

www.ingramcontent.com/pod-product-compliance
Lightning Source LLC
Chambersburg PA
CBHW061459210726
48287CB00007B/2585